HOW THE EWOKS SAVED THE TREES

An Old Ewok Legend

STAR.WARS.

RETURN OF THE JEDI
™

HOW THE EWOKS SAVED THE TREES

An Old Ewok Legend

By James Howe
Illustrated by Walter Velez

Random House 🏠 New York

Copyright © 1984 Lucasfilm Ltd. (LFL). All rights reserved under International and Pan-American Copyright Conventions. Published in the United States by Random House, Inc., New York, and simultaneously in Canada by Random House of Canada Limited, Toronto.

Library of Congress Cataloging in Publication Data: Howe, James. How the Ewoks saved the trees. SUMMARY: Wicket and Kneesaa, two furry Ewok children who live on the tiny moon Endor, catch a pair of giant Phlogs in the act of cutting down the ancient forest trees revered by the Ewoks. [1. Fantasy. 2. Trees—Fiction] I. Velez, Walter, ill. II. Title. PZ7.H83727Hn 1984 [Fic] 83-13708 ISBN: 0-394-86129-9 (trade); 0-394-96129-3 (lib. bdg.)

Manufactured in the United States of America   1 2 3 4 5 6 7 8 9 0

Once upon a time there was a tiny moon called Endor. It was so small in its galaxy of planets and stars that most space travelers whizzed right by without ever knowing it was there. Or if they chanced to notice it, they just continued on their way, not wanting to waste their time on such an unimportant puffball of a moon.

But had they cared to visit Endor, they would have discovered a moon alive with things both big and small. For despite its size, Endor boasted the tallest, most beautiful forest in all the galaxy. The trees were so high that their tops could barely be seen. And sometimes they couldn't be seen at all! Thick vines hung from the trees, and huge ferns, sweet-smelling pine needles, and wildflowers carpeted the forest floor.

Living in the great forest was a race of small, furry creatures called Ewoks. With bright, shiny eyes and black button noses, the Ewoks were as lovable in appearance as they were by nature. They were also very clever.

They lived in huts made of mud and sticks nestled in the high trees of the great forest. Here they busied themselves with many tasks: building homes, planting and harvesting their crops, teaching their children, and making tools and dishes and musical instruments from stone and bark and clay. Each night they gathered around the big bonfire in the center of the village, where they talked of the day's events, sang old Ewok songs, and danced until it grew very late and was time to go to sleep.

Before going off to their hammocks, however, they chanted their thanks to the trees that surrounded them. For to the Ewoks, the trees were living spirits who watched over and protected them. And indeed, the trees in the Endor forest were very unusual. For unlike trees anywhere else in the galaxy, they could speak! Their language was one that only young Ewoks could hear or understand, however. As the Ewoks grew older, the language became less clear, until, when they were fully grown, it was lost to them forever.

This is the story of two young Ewoks, Wicket and Princess Kneesaa, who once had a great adventure in the forest of tall trees. It started late one afternoon as they were gathering berries quite far from their village.

"Whew!" said Wicket, mopping his brow. "I've never picked so many berries. I don't think one or two would be missed, do you?"

Princess Kneesaa laughed as she watched her friend dig hungrily into his basket of juicy red fruit.

"If you eat them at that rate," she said, "you won't have any to take home."

Wicket laughed too. He knew Kneesaa was probably right. She usually was. In no time at all his face was covered with berry juice.

"We should start back soon," Kneesaa said. "It's getting late."

Just then they heard a soft, low moan in the distance, like the sound of someone in pain. Wicket and Kneesaa perked up their ears.

"What is it?" Kneesaa asked.

Wicket shrugged and shook his head.

Then a strange thing happened. The sound swept through the forest like a wind and wrapped itself around the two young Ewoks.

A shudder went up Wicket's spine. What on Endor could be making such a sad, sad noise? Where was it coming from?

Then they heard another sound:

"*Thunk!*"

And again. "*Thunk!*"

It was like something being struck with great force.

"*Thunk! Thunk!*"

Steady and even, it came from far away.

"Let's find out what it is," said Wicket, motioning to Princess Kneesaa to follow. Leaving their baskets, they crept quietly through the forest. The sound grew louder and louder with each step they took.

At last they came to a clearing.

"*THUNK!*"

The sound was very loud now. Wicket and Kneesaa pushed aside a cluster of leaves. What they saw made them gasp.

Two giants, not as tall as the trees but taller than any creatures the two young Ewoks had ever seen or imagined, were chopping down a tree with a mighty ax. Wicket and Kneesaa looked at each other in horror. It was against the Ewok religion to ever hurt the ancient trees, much less to chop one down. They looked back at the fearsome giants and wondered what would happen to them if they were discovered. They would have run away then and there, but if they did, the giants might hear them. The safest thing to do was to stay hidden.

Crouching down, they watched as first one giant, then the other, took great swings at the tree with the ax. It was hard work, and for all the times the ax hit the tree, it seemed to make little more than a dent. The two giants stopped and, wiping their foreheads, turned to each other to speak.

Wicket and Kneesaa listened in amazement to the strange mumbo jumbo that tumbled from the giants' mouths. They had never heard a language such as this before. Its harshness made them wince; its meaning was a total mystery.

Before long the giants picked up their ax and began once again to strike the tree. With every *thunk* of the ax there followed a low moan like the one Wicket and Kneesaa had heard before.

After a while one giant yawned and pointed toward the setting sun. Wicket shivered as he realized that the air had grown cooler. It was getting late and they were far from home. Just as he was wondering when it would be safe to leave, the two giants stretched out their long arms and lay down to sleep, leaving their ax stuck in the tree. Soon Wicket and Kneesaa heard a deep, rumbling snore. The giants were fast asleep.

Quickly Wicket and Kneesaa ran back through the forest, stopping only to pick up their berry baskets. Just then the sad, low moan came through the trees and wrapped itself around the young Ewoks.

"It's the trees!" said Princess Kneesaa.

"Yes," Wicket said. "And it sounds as if they're crying!"

Then the trees began to speak. As Wicket and Kneesaa listened in amazement, the trees told them everything they had learned from the two giants. The giants, the trees explained, came from a land known as Simoom on the other side of the moon of Endor. Once, long ago, there had been a forest in Simoom, but now it was a great, dry desert.

What became of the forest? Wicket wanted to know.

The Phlogs—for this was what these giant creatures were called—had cut down all the trees in Simoom to make a palace for their king. Now, said the trees, who heard it from the Phlogs, the palace had burned to the ground and the king had ordered his subjects to build him a new one. But there were no longer any trees in Simoom. And that is why the two Phlogs had come to this forest. They had been sent on a mission to find trees. Soon they would go home. And then they would return with other Phlogs to cut down the trees in the Ewoks' forest.

When the trees had finished telling their story, they began to cry again. Wicket and Kneesaa looked at each other, not sure what to do, but certain that something must be done—and soon.

Grabbing their baskets, they ran through the forest until they came to their village. Then they went at once to the hut of Chief Chirpa, who was not only chief of all the Ewoks but was Kneesaa's father as well.

"Father!" cried Kneesaa when she saw the chief. "Wait until we tell you what we've seen!"

And then Kneesaa and Wicket, in a jumble of words that spilled out of their mouths as fast as they could think them, told Chief Chirpa about the two Phlogs and their great ax and all that the trees had told them.

Chief Chirpa nodded slowly as he listened. When the young Ewoks had finished, he stood up and said, "I will call a meeting of the elders. You will tell them what you have just told me."

Soon all the elders of the village arrived at Chief
Chirpa's hut. The chief sat on a throne made of twigs and
vines and instructed the children to speak.

At first Wicket felt shy. He had never spoken to the
Council of Elders before. But it was not long before he was
telling his tale with great gusto. Every once in a while
Princess Kneesaa tried to put in a word or two, but Wicket
was racing on so breathlessly that she found it almost
impossible to say a thing.

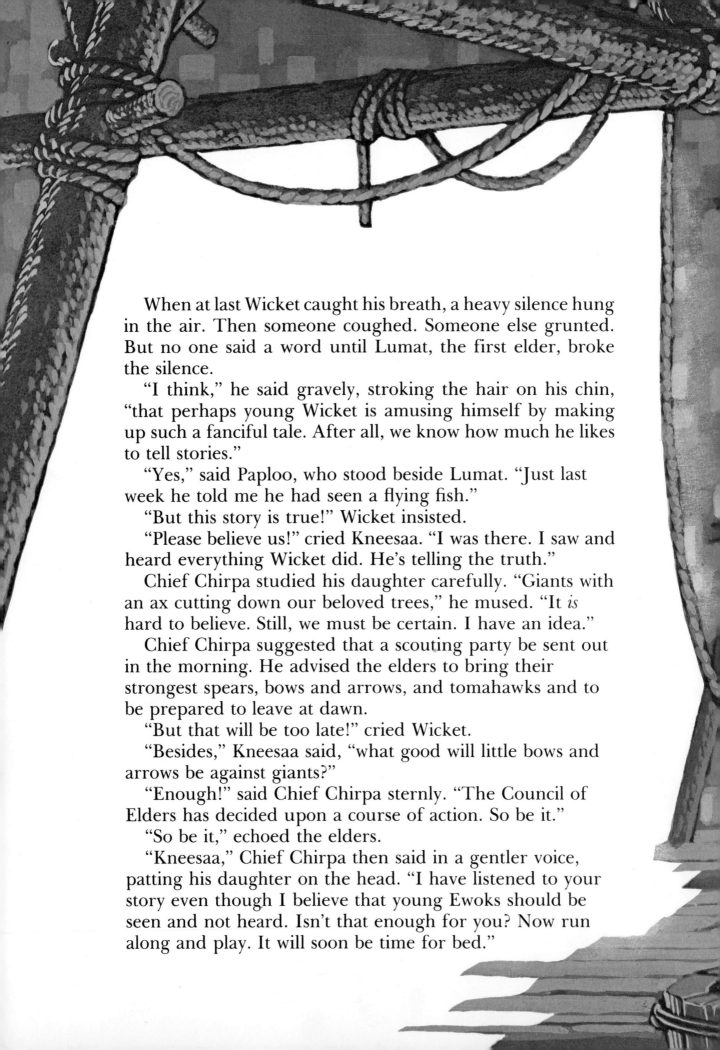

When at last Wicket caught his breath, a heavy silence hung in the air. Then someone coughed. Someone else grunted. But no one said a word until Lumat, the first elder, broke the silence.

"I think," he said gravely, stroking the hair on his chin, "that perhaps young Wicket is amusing himself by making up such a fanciful tale. After all, we know how much he likes to tell stories."

"Yes," said Paploo, who stood beside Lumat. "Just last week he told me he had seen a flying fish."

"But this story is true!" Wicket insisted.

"Please believe us!" cried Kneesaa. "I was there. I saw and heard everything Wicket did. He's telling the truth."

Chief Chirpa studied his daughter carefully. "Giants with an ax cutting down our beloved trees," he mused. "It *is* hard to believe. Still, we must be certain. I have an idea."

Chief Chirpa suggested that a scouting party be sent out in the morning. He advised the elders to bring their strongest spears, bows and arrows, and tomahawks and to be prepared to leave at dawn.

"But that will be too late!" cried Wicket.

"Besides," Kneesaa said, "what good will little bows and arrows be against giants?"

"Enough!" said Chief Chirpa sternly. "The Council of Elders has decided upon a course of action. So be it."

"So be it," echoed the elders.

"Kneesaa," Chief Chirpa then said in a gentler voice, patting his daughter on the head. "I have listened to your story even though I believe that young Ewoks should be seen and not heard. Isn't that enough for you? Now run along and play. It will soon be time for bed."

"Run along and play," Wicket muttered as he and Kneesaa left the chief's hut. "They don't understand! Grownups never do!"

"*I* know!" Kneesaa said suddenly. "Let's talk to Logray. He'll know what we should do."

"That's a great idea!" Wicket agreed.

And the two Ewoks set off to visit their friend Logray, the oldest Ewok of their tribe. Logray lived by himself in a little hut on the far edge of the village. For years he'd kept pretty much to himself. It wasn't that he didn't like the other Ewoks or that they didn't like him; it was more that no one knew quite what to make of Logray. He was the only one of the older Ewoks who still understood the language of the trees. In fact, he seemed to know more about many things than did any of the other Ewoks. Some thought he was a wizard. A few admitted that they were afraid of him. But none of these were children. For the young Ewoks loved Logray and spent hours of their time with him. As for the grownup Ewoks, their paths crossed Logray's only when they were sick, for he was always able to cure them with his special healing herbs and powders.

That night Logray did not speak for a long time after Wicket and Kneesaa had told him their story. He just settled back in his chair and stared into the darkness outside his window. The young Ewoks exchanged a look: Had they been wrong to think Logray would be able to help them?

Finally, letting out a great sigh, Logray turned to face Wicket and Kneesaa. He looked deeply into their eyes as he spoke.

"The trees were correct," he said. "The Phlogs do come from the other side of Endor. But what they did not tell you is that the Phlogs endanger not only our precious trees but our very lives as well."

At that moment a forest bird hooted in the still night air and made both Wicket and Kneesaa jump.

"I will tell you a story," Logray went on, "one long forgotten by most Ewoks. It was told to me by my own grandfather when I was a child.

"Many, many years ago, long before you or your parents or grandparents, or even your great-grandparents, were born, the Ewoks lived on the other side of Endor, in the land known as Simoom. They did not make their home in the desert—for to this day Ewoks cannot bear the heat of the desert sun—but in a small patch of green, the only forest in all of Simoom. Here the trees protected them not only from the sun but from the Phlogs who lived in the desert around them.

"One day the Phlogs decided to build a palace for their king. They looked around and saw that there was only one material from which to build: the tall, strong trees of the forest. They chopped them all down in no time at all, leaving the Ewoks open to the burning rays of the sun and, worse, to the whims of the big and powerful Phlogs. Under the cover of night, the Ewoks fled the place that had been their home for many, many years. By day they tried to find shelter from the sun. By night they continued their journey. After many days and nights had passed, they reached the edge of Simoom and found that the other side of the moon of Endor was a lush, green forest. Here they settled and here they have lived in peace and comfort from that day until this."

Logray turned his gaze to the window, once more lost in thought. The bird hooted again in the darkness, but this time neither Wicket nor Kneesaa jumped, for they were under the spell of Logray's story.

"Now the Phlogs are back among us," Logray said in his deep voice. "If we wait for the scouting party to go out in the morning, it may be too late. I have a plan. It will be difficult and very dangerous and it may not work, but you must try. Take this powder and put it into the Phlogs' food while they are sleeping. When they eat it, they will forget everything they have seen on this side of Endor—including the trees. Instead, they will believe that this is an enchanted place, full of danger to all the Phlogs. They will leave, vowing never to return."

Logray gave Wicket and Kneesaa each a small sack of white powder and bid them hurry into the forest before the Phlogs awakened.

Clutching their sacks tightly, the young Ewoks said good-bye to their friend Logray and ran quickly across the bridge that separated his hut from the rest of the village. Suddenly Wicket came to a halt.

"Watch out," he whispered to Kneesaa. "We don't want our parents to see us."

But it was too late.

"So there you are," cried Wicket's mother in the distance. She was holding a lamp aloft. "I've been looking all over for you. Kneesaa, your father wants you to go right home."

Sadly the two young Ewoks looked at each other. What were they to do now?

"We'll meet in the morning," Kneesaa suggested, "before the sun comes up. Sneak out of your bed and meet me at the bridge. If we're lucky, we'll get to the Phlogs before they wake up."

"Don't let your father see your sack of magic powder," Wicket said. Reluctantly the two friends said good night and went off to their beds.

Wicket and Kneesaa hardly slept that night. They couldn't wait until the first glimmer of dawn, when their daring adventure would begin. They were afraid, but excited too.

At last they crawled out of their beds and crept silently through the village to meet at the bridge near Logray's hut.

"Let's go," Wicket whispered when he spotted Kneesaa.

Together they made their way through the dense forest until they came to the clearing where they'd left the Phlogs. The sun was just beginning to rise. From the deep snores that shook the ground under their feet, they knew the Phlogs were still asleep.

"We'll have to hurry," Kneesaa said in a hush. "We don't have much time."

"Look!" said Wicket. He pointed to a large bag that was lying on the ground several yards from the sleeping giants. "I'll bet their food is in there."

Without a sound Wicket and Kneesaa crawled toward the bag. But just as Kneesaa was about to lift up the flap, Wicket's knee snapped a branch in two.

"C-r-rack!" went the branch.

The Phlogs' great eyes popped open. Immediately they spotted Wicket and Kneesaa. One of the giants just grumbled sleepily. But the other arched his eyebrows menacingly and broke into a big grin.

"Run!" cried Wicket.

Wicket and Kneesaa started to run away as fast as their legs could carry them. But the Phlogs simply stretched out their arms and scooped the tiny Ewoks up into their enormous hands. Holding their prizes tightly, they rose to their feet.

The Phlog who had captured Wicket sniffed the Ewok curiously, then held him next to his ear and shook him, as if to see what was inside.

The other Phlog smiled as he looked at the frightened princess in his hand. He mumbled a few words in his strange, harsh language, then licked Kneesaa, as if to find out how she tasted.

"Ick!" said Kneesaa as the long, thick tongue rolled over her.

"Princess!" Wicket cried. "We've got to act fast before they eat us for breakfast! When I count to three, we'll throw our powder into their faces. Ready? One . . . two . . . three!"

Together Wicket and Kneesaa tossed the contents of the sacks Lograg had given them into the Phlogs' faces. At first nothing happened. The two Phlogs just looked startled. Both of them sneezed, just once, and then they dropped the Ewoks to the ground and began to rub their faces, trying to wipe off the fine, white powder. Then, looking very confused, they became still. And a moment later they crumpled slowly to the ground and fell into a deep, deep sleep.

Wicket and Kneesaa wanted to believe that Logray's powder had worked, but at the moment they were too scared to believe anything. Just seconds before, they had been clutched in the fists of two hungry Phlogs, their lives hanging in the balance! Now they turned and ran into the forest to hide.

Cowering behind a large fern, they thought they were finally safe when suddenly they heard: "Crunch! Crunch! Crunch!" They looked at each other. Were more Phlogs coming to get them? They closed their eyes and held their breath.

"What are you two doing here?"

It was Chief Chirpa's voice. Wicket and Kneesaa opened their eyes to see the Ewok scouting party standing before them. They let out great sighs of relief.

Princess Kneesaa explained everything. Then she and Wicket took the elders into the clearing and showed them the two slumbering giants.

"So what you told us was indeed true," Chief Chirpa said, nodding his head.

"But what if Logray's powder doesn't work?" asked Lumat. "After all, he is a bit strange. He may have told Wicket and Kneesaa a story just to get them to leave him alone."

"Logray isn't like that!" protested Kneesaa.

"His powder will work," Wicket said. "It just has to."

Paploo stepped forward and drew an arrow from his quiver. "*I* will take care of these giants," he boasted. He drew back his bow string and sent the arrow flying. Everyone watched as the arrow whistled through the air and landed with a "ping" on the arm of one of the sleeping Phlogs. It didn't even make a scratch. Instead it just bounced off the giant's thick hide and fell to the ground.

Embarrassed, Paploo muttered something to himself and withdrew.

"Well," said Lumat, "it looks as if our weapons are useless against them. I have another idea. Let's tie them up. At least that way we'll be safe until we figure out what to do next."

"Unless they break free," said Wicket softly.

No one said anything then because they didn't want to
believe that what Wicket suggested could actually happen.
Instead, they hurriedly began to cut down vines and chop
up bits of dead wood. When they had gathered all that
they needed, they stretched the vines across the
mountainous bodies of the Phlogs and tied them securely
to the wooden pegs they had driven into the ground. It
took them almost an hour to finish the job, and when they
were done, they were very tired.

The Ewok elders leaned back against the trunks of the
trees to rest. All at once Princess Kneesaa cried out, "Look!
They're waking up!"

Everyone shrank back as the two fallen giants opened their eyes. Their brows furrowed, they rolled their heads from side to side as if trying to make sense of where they were and how it was that they found themselves waking up a second time that morning. Grunting, they tugged at the vines strapped across their chests. Would they hold? At first it seemed as if they would. But then, with little more effort than it would take an Ewok to brush aside a cobweb, the Phlogs broke through the vines and sat up.

The hearts of the Ewoks sank. What would happen to them once the Phlogs realized they were there?

But then the look of confusion in the giants' eyes changed to one of fear. They pointed wildly at the trees and staggered to their feet. Without even noticing the Ewoks, they turned and ran off into the forest as if they were being chased by demons.

The cries of the Phlogs pierced the air as they ran. Only the trees understood what they were saying. The trees told Wicket and Kneesaa, who in turn told the elders.

"A strange and evil land!" the Phlogs had cried. "We must hurry home and never return!" Logray's magic powder had worked!

As the Phlogs grew smaller and smaller in the distance, the sound of music filled the forest. At first only Wicket and Kneesaa could hear it.

"It's the trees!" they shouted. "They're singing their thanks to us!"

When Wicket and Kneesaa told them this, the elders bowed down to the trees. And then the music became so loud and so sweet that everyone could hear it, even the Ewoks back in the village.

"A miracle!" they cried. "A miracle has taken place in the forest!"

That night the Ewoks gathered around the bonfire to celebrate their victory over the Phlogs. Logray, coaxed out of his hut, was named Medicine Man, and Wicket and Kneesaa were made honorary members of the Council of Elders, the first time in the tribe's history that Ewoks so young had been given such an honor.

Everyone sang and danced until late into the night.
Then Chief Chirpa pounded his staff against the earth and
silenced the joyous Ewoks. "Every year," he proclaimed,
"during the first moon of summer, we will travel to the
clearing where we defeated the Phlogs and give thanks."

And to this day the Ewoks go every year to the clearing and bow down before the tree that still bears the mark of the Phlogs' ax. And as the trees sing a melody that can be heard by young and old, the Ewoks chant these words:

Trees and Ewoks,
Ewoks and Trees,
Always will we help each other.
Always will we live as one.

And that is how, once upon a time on a tiny moon called Endor, the Ewoks saved the trees.